I0519519

Sunbathing

in

Winnemucca

Kurt Rasmussen

Binary Press 2014

Acknowledgements

Thanks, K, for publishing this thing.

Thank you, Megan, for being my eyes outside of the balloon; I couldn't have asked for a better editor.

Thank you, Axel and Lena, for putting up with a crazy father like me.

Thank you, Neena, Joy, Annika, Charice and my other poet friends for listening and sharing.

Thank you, Stanislav Petrov, for not blowing up the fucking world.

I guess that's about it.

To JulieAnn, sister of my soul

Contents

sunbathing in winnemucca

I think his real name was Isidro
but he went by Chilo.
Back when a drugstore truck drivin man
sent the unions and OSHA down the shitter;
which is why
in the next scene of this movie
Doug and I are working with an illegal named Chilo
(who was in fact an all right motherfucker)
With his fifty words of English
twelve hours a day
standing in the scoop of a front loader
knee deep in concrete holding buckets.
But then Chilo leaned too far
pouring his bucket into the wall
and fell the fuck out.

I saw that he didn't land on his head at least,
but there was a two-by-four under him
and he sat up holding his side
so we figured a broken rib.

The boss said, "Better take him down to Winnemucca."

So that's how we found ourselves;
me and Doug in front,
Chilo in back,
passing a bottle of Jim Beam,
ZZ Top and the hot air blasting
with pissed-off crows
lifting with reluctance
off of road kill on the egg-frying asphalt
as we hauled our asses by.
And I looked back at Chilo
and he smiled okay
and I handed him the bottle

and Doug called out:
"Now that place up there
they used to have whores
and they could still do."

I say, "Well I have to piss anyway
and probly so does Chilo."
We walk in the place blinking
because we can't see shit
until finally we make out
a couple guys at the bar and a woman
who indeed looks very whore-like.

So I hit the john
and piss on the urinal cake
looking at:
'nothing could be finer
than to be in her vaginer'
written in red marker on the wall,
and I think it probably isn't talking
about that woman at the bar
who Doug has sidled up to in my absence
which is okay with me
cause no amount of condom
is going to make that shit okay.

Chilo's smile is kinda forced
so I say, "Let's hit the fuckin road."
But Doug just keeps on
talking to her highness,
so I say it again.
He throws me the keys and says,
"Collect me on your way back."
I say, "Well, whatever's left of you, maybe."
And I wink at Chilo,
and then we're back on the road.

Ten minutes go by
and we're about five miles from the freeway
(which means twenty miles from town)
when the engine cuts out
and I look down at the gauge and say,
"That stupid fuckin Doug motherfucker."

I manage to pull over before it dies.

I say, "Well, what about it, Chilo?"
who is still in fact smiling
even with that blood
at the corner
of his mouth.

I get out and stand in the road
in that blazing August sun.
It's just me and the crows
and maybe God,
I don't know.

These days I'll likely stop
when I see a man waving
even if he's
someone like me.

Part 1

correct emotions I

I have never been able to feel correct emotions;
I'm feeling a wrong emotion right now, in fact,
so you might want your money back for this poem.
You will say that there are no correct emotions,
you will say it with a hint of a condescending smile
and you will be a little proud of yourself for saying it.
Just as you were back in first grade, remember?
When you raised your hand and got the right answer?
And the teacher said, "Yes, that's right Mary Alice!"
Except it wasn't fucking right. Was it, Mary Alice?

No, even there in first grade you could sense
the importance of feeling correct emotions,
as when our teacher, Mrs. Barnes (remember her?)
kept making Bernard try to read the word, 'bottle'?
But he wasn't going to read that word on the chalkboard;
not Bernard, whom the bus brought each morning
from his basque hovel somewhere in the sagebrush.
Where they ate nothing but the testicles of sheep
(or at least that's what we whispered to each other).
Do you remember, Mary Alice, how we all laughed?
Mrs. Barnes kept yelling, "Just sound it out!"
And Bernard kept saying, "baa...baa...baa..."
and Mrs. Barnes said, "Well, you are what you eat!"
and we laughed and laughed and laughed and laughed.

I remember leaning forward on my wooden desk
in a spasm of merciless communal mirth.
I remember feeling the correct emotion that day
like a hot wire from my nuts to my heart, we all felt it.
What a stupid name anyway: Bernard, Bernard;
he smelled like sour milk and he never looked up.
That fucking dumb Bernard. Where is he now?

The truth is I don't care if he's alive or dead.
I wish we'd stood up for him a little bit, though;
not because he deserved it with his stupid name
and his eating of testicles and his sour smell,
but because Mrs. Barnes was clearly the enemy.
We should have surged from our desks and swarmed
like a gaggle of savage geese in blue bonnets,
with ginsu knife teeth and deodorant breath,
biting chunks out of her big fat teacher ass
and eating them just like Bernard ate testicles.
Do you remember how fat she was, Mary Alice?
Each buttock far bigger than poor, stinky Bernard.

But no, even then we sensed how things worked;
we knew what was what, what we had to do.
What chance did a room full of first-graders have?
We could never devour that fat fist in a dress
who led us each morning in our pledge to the flag.
To swallow her would be to swallow the whole world.
But Bernard from the sagebrush was just little - like a testicle
the correct thing to do was to devour him;
so that's what we did, Mary Alice, you and I.
And then later I made a meal out of you,
and you spent two decades swallowing me.
And each night our mouths came correctly together
with a carrion stench of testicles on our breath.

sapphires in the mud

I have inhaled the musk-soaked wind of your legend
until my lungs are sagging like old water skins,
for you are goddess to the lost tribe of cannibals
foraging in the wet gray folds of my brain.

You know that we will not lie here again,
bare-ass naked on a thrift store bed sheet,
the road map for a hundred old love-journeys,
conspiring against logic in our language of touch.

To ask for continuance is to ask for too much.
The stems of old roses are deadwood now;
new blooms devoured them with bloody teeth:
this is the hard grammar in which life is expressed.

It is the transient pleasures that we all love best.
your father stacked hay bales for half a year
to spend three minutes holding your mother's breast.
We are each the result of ten seconds of bliss.

But this poem is just nothing if that's all there is.
Cold-eyed conduits channeling power to reduce us:
the marketplace carries no energy here.
Something from these afternoons will persist.

They are hard like jewels, they will always exist.
They are sapphires trampled into the wet ground
by all the feet of the migrating sufferers.
I will carry them in a leather bag on my heart.

ah my friend

Ah my friend to think of you being here,
waiting for me by the lake, when only last night
we got way too drunk at the bar.
Then later outside the hotel,
you were telling me something
and I nodded my head
to show I understood.
But suddenly nodding my head
seemed like the best trick in the world
and I confess-

I wasn't listening to your sodden drone because
My God! I have a head!
And I can nod it like some miracle
and I realized that this is mind over matter because look:
Hey head *move!*
And it fucking moved!
Hey move again... *NOW!*
And I felt the electric spasm of my thought
move through my meat and bone.
I'm just this rump roast that moves
with an idea and a will.
I'm a piece of a crazy, drooling, idiot, shitting-his-pants God
infusing this meat.

Yet, I am not the meat,
Though the meat moves; the action of nodding my head
became a work of art in a godful dance.
A fist in the face of nothing.
Because I am here and moving this head
and I will forever nod in slow syncopation
to your words,
all of them dripping full with meaning to you-
yet only a rhythmic, pulsing, mucous-flapping-drone to me.
"Sorry sorry, sorry baby," you say

"lets swim naked in the lake!"
I say, "Of course my love!"
(although by 'love' I mean some rodent-eyed thing
which peers from a hole)
To the lake we go!
Both knowing it's nuts,
drunkenness notwithstanding, but
it's a matter of principle now.

Yes, we will swim in that lake
and I intend to fuck you in it,
Pounding lake water like a pile driver into your wincing hole.
Meeting perhaps a ragged-toothed eel
(at this point I can only speculate)
But we finally reach the shore,
and each with a criminal squint at the other
we shed our clothes and dive down.
We pull ourselves down with powerful arm-strokes
and I am breathing no problem,
and I look at you stroking beside me,
and see the delicate fringe of your gills.
and know that I have them too.

Down down down we reach the bottom
and find skeletons caught in old barbed wire
with scuba gear hanging ragged silent from the bones
and we both know it is time for our coupling.
Catfish look on with their sucking mouths
and depthless insane fish eyes,
and you are this enormous crawfish now-
you grip me with your claws,
and I am a man again
and I can't breath.

I am drowning as you gently rub
your soft under-tail on my groin.
It feels impossibly good.

The orgasm burns
I am dying, dying.
Your eyes are on stalks now;
they are staring into mine.
My mouth snaps open carp-like
sending murky silver trains of light toward the surface

be flat blues

My thoughts keep going inside this stone
that lives in my pocket-
but there is no room in there.
There is no space inside a stone.

My thoughts are pressed as flat as a B-flat
played by a drawing of a saxophone,
described in a novella
that someone plans to write.

I've heard people talk about delving into centers.
I should introduce them to my friend 'Stone'.
He would press their penetration into
a sheet of gas between his grains.

Actually there's a city inside my stone,
the streets of which are walked by my thoughts
which have poor posture and speak in surly mumbles
on street corners late into the night.

My stone might be a heart of stone.
Which on second thought can't be in a poem now
under strictly enforced federal law,
so never mind.

Really the thing is: I believe I left
a thought about you in my stone
the last time I was there.

The perfect place for it I think.

Its name is 'Goodbye'.

one day
(A poem for the new year for my PFMW friends)

One day the walls will finish closing in.
I'll cough out the last of the usual lies like
hairballs made of old thrift shop rags.
My imaginary lover will be a splay-toothed rodent
chewing through my chest with hungry squeaks
and I'll suddenly get the colossal joke of thinking
that I could have done anything different.

One day I will smell the gun-metal breath
of my killer's wet face close to mine
and he'll smile at me sadly with fish-belly eyes
while pushing hot steel into my squirming heart
and only as the black stain of life leaks away
will I know that he is a ghost of my own contrivance.

One day I will squander my last roll of the bones
to assuage the blunt beaks of a buzzard circle.
I will channel the dregs of my sole sacred spirit
into the smoking bullet-molds of the blind consensus.

But today isn't one day.

Today is only now.

Strange to find myself here in this instant with you,
possessing still the wherewithal and the inclination
to meet this next acid moment in such royal company.
People talk about the chances of things happening.
My inflatable dollar store buddha once told me,
the chances of any single state of affairs
coming to pass are basically zero, yet here we are.

Friends, I sat down to write you a fancy poem today.
Something with layers, a trick ending, special effects.
Hidden trap doors leading to troves of insight.
A pretty girl maybe, even a car chase or two.
But I just keep finding ways to say the same thing.

Every life and every poem is an answer to one question.
One day there isn't going to be a one day.

So what are you going to do

Now?

lines found on a rooftop as darkness fell

The stopped spirit deposits an orbital
in the hallway of some downtown building
quiet, but for the sixty hertz hum,
exactly like outer space.

You might pass a human being there
in your quantum state of silence
whose eyes do not meet yours, but only
dart from throat to chest to shoulder.
Like the nervous red dot of a roof top gun.

It's long since the thing should have fallen;
Eyes wide like a psychotic cow,
milked by blind robotic lobsters,
a stray bullet from the daily swat team,
piercing its fat black heart.

But the beast, unaccountably, lumbers on
grazing on the severed penises
of unemployed corporate accountants
and the hot torn hearts of lunatic whores.

It would have been better if we'd never met.
If I'd never done the double-take
on your insane caged raptor eyes.
Never made love in the beast's fourth stomach
among the drunk janitor's empty bottles
while the steam train ballerina danced
into the greedy fingers of the night.

corners

Doing some cleaning today, I text her.
"Don't forget the corners," she replies.

Uneasiness blooms like an inner rash.
So... she's been looking at my corners.

I scan my interior now, with borrowed eyes
and find a hundred dirty corners
regarding me like little policemen
wanting to step on my punk face.

How could I have lived here all this time,
daily breaking the beams of these glares
and hear no alarms going off?

Another failure, it must be owned.
More work for my inner PR man.

My dwelling is now a hostile enclosure
a fever-hot abscess rejecting my existence.
The thought of simply moving out
is quickly dismissed, but it does come up,
as does a twinge of scalp-taking rage.

I consider possible courses of action:
I could Turn Over a New Leaf,
become an earnest student of clean corners,
The Clean Corner Guy, Mister Clean-Corner.

But would this not betray my very personhood?
I mean, exactly what kind of whore am I here?

No, fuck it, no, I will embrace my dark corners!
Without them I would be mere office equipment.
Something to be rented out, bought and sold,
a vending machine of vacuous smalltalk.

My corners will grow along the walls and ceilings
like veins of black poisonous blood,
covering every surface with defiant gore.

But what I really do is neither of these.

I walk from room to room, bending over,
tenderly touching all of my corners
as though each one was a leaking wound.

suburban sunset

I don't see anyone walking out there beyond the lake,
casting thirty-mile shadows into my boyhood cigar box,
to whom I might yell through an old toilet paper roll, asking
for something to keep in the mind's vest pocket,
safe from the judgments of all dive-bombing shitbirds.

I'm thinking of some cave in those sunset mountains
where a man once thought of his woman and his children
while he lay in the cool dust and looked out at the stars.
His moccasins and his fire tools might be there still.
Let this poem be the terminus of my dead brother's journey.

first date #1023

Hello.

Thank you for looking more-or-less like your photos.
Actually you seem even more attractive
than your pictures portray you.
And that is highly unusual.
I like to think the same is true of me
but I could easily be deceiving myself.
I seem to do that quite often.

After getting our coffee, we sit on faux leather cushions
which make sounds like weary sighs
as we press our buttocks into them.

I think about your buttocks.

We tell each other a little about our lives.
Children, jobs, hobbies, et cetera.
We could be lying through our teeth, of course,
though I, for one, am far from being skilled enough
to compose a falsehood so elaborately mundane,
so relentlessly typical,
and I suspect the same is true of you.

No.

We are are truth-tellers, you and I, sitting here.
Tellers of small truths, or
Farting, fucking, weeping, dying machines
through which the truth is made small.

Truth compactors.

A mother walks by,
leading a completely bald child in an apparent trance.
A cancer victim, no doubt, I think;

and a very brave one for not concealing that hideous,
vaguely amphibious-looking head.
Of course, these are my savage interior thoughts
that I would never share with you.
Both of us watch the thing pass without remark.

Turning back to you
with what I hope is not a creepy smile,
I inwardly speculate as to what
your breasts must look like naked.
This is an old habit
that I've tried to conceal over the years
with perhaps only modest success;
my apologies, ma'am.
Please feel free to similarly evaluate
the protrusion of my gut over my belt
when I go to refill my coffee cup.
The physical side of things
is important, let's admit.
We are mammals, after all.
Albeit far beyond the age, you and I,
to which our ancestors
of the paleolithic age,
would normally have lived,
let alone contemplate
such frivolous nonsense as 'romance',
which is what we're seeking here.

Aren't we?

But we can already tell, can't we,
that you and I are not going to fall in love.
I can't really say what the trouble is;
certainly you are attractive enough,
but for some mysterious reason
I just can't imagine myself
caring very deeply about you

and I'm quite certain that you feel
the same way about me;
in fact I'm willing to grant
that your lack of caring is prior to
and perhaps even causative of my own.

If we are, unbeknownst to me,
engaged in some contest of ennui
I am more than willing
to concede you the winner.
I'm that much of a gentleman, at least.
A lack of chemistry, I suppose,
is what we have here.

But we're only fifteen minutes into our date and,
judging by your pleasant
(if somewhat distracted) smile
which is the twin sibling of my own, no doubt,
and by the content of these words
that seem to keep dropping from our mouths
like turds from a pink-eyed lab rat's ass,
neither of us has any intention of just walking away
and good on us for that, I say;
at least we're both far too nice for that.

That's all right, ma'am.
I wish you well in your endeavors
which I will only share for the next hour or so
and we will smile and talk and maybe laugh
until it will not seem too awkward to say goodnight
and I might even softly brush my lips upon yours.
But for now I will imagine us in some paleolithic cave,
entwined together beside a fire of mammoth dung,
ten thousand years before love was invented.

morning prayer

6 a.m. in the Wyoming gut-shot morning.
The broke-footed waitress in pelican drag
smiles to dole out her tired morning lips
left swimming in my coffee like
suffocating crimson tadpoles, so I
try to read my book.
But the words are in some foreign tongue now,
they mean only: grab the river-soaked rag doll
and tie her off with a dexterous dangle
fun fun fun-fun-FUN!!
And that's when I look up
and see the bearded hole
chewing like the wincing sphincter
on my future's hairy bung
which I worry about falling into
and I fleetingly see myself tying
a 2×4 across my ass
to prevent this.
Amen.

goodbye #37

What if our histories were visible
like the blur in a slow shutter photo?
We'd be these centipedes with human segments
crawling through the shit heap of space-time.
To understand where you've been
I'd just look down the worm-like length of you
clear back to your newborn ass.

But that's not how it is.
All I know is what you're telling me.
Those wary, preoccupied eyes
and the way you flinch sometimes
like some ghost is slapping you
and how you answer any personal question
as though
you're in the twelfth hour of interrogation
commencing your false confession.

Who knows what our time-worms will look like
a couple of years down the line?
All I know is
they will not be intertwined
as they might have been.

But my advisers are telling me
that this is no grounds for sadness,
and are urging me not to give a fuck-
so I guess that's what I'll do.

But anyway,

since this is the only poem of mine
you will ever visit
you should get all dolled-up
for this last stanza.

Show me those sexy legs
one last time,
and flash those spooky dark eyes
just once more
and don your very finest alluring smile
as a parting gift.
Because photoshop
ain't got nothing on poetry, baby,
and trust me:
neither of us will ever look so good again.

the rescue

Why do you want to shut me up?

My words are not your plastic doll heads
dropping dead-eyed from my stuttering mouth,
and you will not devour them today.
No.
So hands off.
Fuck you.
I'm scared too, but
your face is this ballooning mask.
I grab it with my fists;
two fistfuls of your boiling mud-pot face
and I pull and pull and pull but
I am the only one that's hurting.

I am walking down an endless hall
so clean except for gutters of blood.
I am trying to act casual.
The air is viscous like silent water
at the bottom of a dark, dark sea.
People are looking at me;
one is a naked grandmother
breastfeeding a pair of hagfish.
My smile is a closed blowhole.
My face says I have business,
yes.
I am supposed to be here;
gotta carry out my mission.

You are crazy.
I'm rescuing you.
I pissed on the electric fence to short it out.
Yes, it burned my dick but
I got past it, didn't I?
Now I'm in the building where they keep you.

Gonna try to bust you out.
I have no plan but I gotta do this.
A woman looks at me,
I make eye-contact because
acting casual entails wanting to fuck to her,
just as I would if I were a real man;
a human man instead of this other thing.

Trying to find you,
I can't.
I could ask the security guy.
I could ask, "excuse me sir -
but where do they keep the crazy women?
Crazy from having their hearts gouged out
again and again and again?"
Yes, I'm to blame.
Yes, I'm the murder weapon, but
I have no mind of my own, I am only a tool;
a tool in the hands of retarded sea gods
bagging groceries with raging hard-ons.

Now I'm on the top floor, the last floor.
I stop and I look out the window,
next to some old fuck whose old lady just died.
Yeah I'm sorry for him.
I really am.
I cry for this man.
I cry gallons of salty liquid.
I howl - I howl for this man's loss.
I grab his bony old shoulders.
I crush him to me I'm so torn up;
I crush him to me.
Then the fear comes into his eyes,
we hear his bones crack like old dry sticks.
Our eyes are one inch apart.
Crack go the bones.

I say "oops."
I drop him.
The bones are all busted.
He's just a puddle of wrinkled skin
like a pool of vomit with a face.
Sorry old man gotta go -

I get to the last door on the top floor
of the last nut-house in the world.
The door's not even locked; I walk in,
I'm crying again.
I say, "I came to get you baby."
I reach my hand out, but
you are now this wild thing of the sea.
You slither up my arm like
some ravenous eel with a thousand teeth,
tearing my flesh.
In a heartbeat you're at my neck.
Bubbles rise merrily from my gaping mouth.
It is so silent here.
You're nothing but eyes and teeth now.
Just two huge mad, mad eyes
over teeth,
devouring my howling throat.

a memory is created

Your curly hair assumes a
prominence at this distance,
like enameled blunt spikes under
my cage-pacing brain.
You are somewhere across this
frozen valley tonight.
Probably sleeping
while I sit up wasting yet another quarter hour
involved in thoughts of you.

But this is it.
you were never more than
an apparition here anyway,
though you might flatter yourself
by supposing otherwise.
Your face is fading already,
leaving only a sharp nose
like a thorn which hurts a little
when my thoughts grasp it.

So now I will put you down in my mind's
cluttered basement,
like a piece of collectible junk
that I picked up somewhere,
thinking it might turn out to be worth
something someday.
Curly hair made of brass wire
over a faceless nub of.... lead?
If the artist is trying to tell me something,
I don't get it.

at the fat chance saloon

Heather digs me and I dig her back.
We are drinking whiskey
at the fat chance saloon.
After shot #2 she tells me
she used to manage a strip club.
She proceeds to appraise
the women around us
with the discerning eye of a professional.
No man would deal out assessments
as brutal as hers, however,
I concur with all of her judgments.

After shot #3 I get that lonely feeling
and think about making love to Heather.
It crosses my mind to ask her
how she would appraise herself
but I know she'd just do it
without missing a beat
and then point her guns at me.
I do wish that she was prettier
and didn't live with that guy.
But then I'm pretty sure she wishes
some shit about me too.

something about being alone

When the sun began coming up, there would
have been a glow in the sky behind me
(if I had existed outside of this poem).
But I would not have seen it because
I was facing forward.
Which was west-
which was the direction I was going.

Looking out over the dead, pale desert land
my eyes feel full of broken glass
and I run a hand over my oily hair
and see the sign for gas up ahead.
So I pull in and get out
and the air is chilly but I know
it will be killing-hot in three hours
so I just be cold to store it up.
I put the nozzle in the tank
and then, I see this face looking at me-
this huge face,
and I see that it's a head that someone has sculpted
out of newspaper and wire and glue
and painted with poster paint.

This huge hollow paper head
higher than my waist. Lying there on its cheek
over there by the big propane tank.
And I wonder who made the goddamn thing
as I stand there pumping gas
thinking of the clever comebacks I will say
to the edge of the world when I get there,
(I can see it gaping only nine lines away)
just before going over
and becoming nothing.
But then a chill morning desert breeze comes up
and I hear it whispering over the dead land.

And it lifts that huge-ass paper head
so that now it is glaring at me, and nodding in the breeze
like it's trying to tell me something.
Maybe the end of this poem I'm in or-
maybe just something about being alone

Part 2

correct emotions II

The next thing I got wrong was this business about god.
I was just a boy, out in the sand and the sagebrush
and I didn't know shit except that you couldn't see God.
Just like you couldn't see love and you couldn't see hate
and you couldn't see the war that people talked about.

But these were the things that brought blood to the faces,
and a dog's yelp and snarl to the voices in my life.
And they were the things that I was learning about then;
God and hate and war and the significance of numbers.
Like the number of dollars that my father brought home,
or the number of dead soldiers that they told us each night,
and the small number that they gave my brother
that made him curse and slam the door and get drunk-
and made my father throw him the length of our trailer
winging him like a tossed doll past my bedroom door
when he came home yelling deep in the night.

But the best number was the number of God, which was one.
And during those few years when I believed
I kept expecting God to look down and notice me
and train a huge magnifying glass on my back
and burn me into oblivion with a puff of smoke.
That's what I would have done, after all;
that's what I *did* do
to the ants that I was God of
out in that lonely land where we lived.
Their red bodies would flail like berserk machines
then wither and curl up into tiny black balls
with a little wisp of acrid smoke.

But then one summer
after a day spent wandering and dreaming in the sagebrush
I came home to our little trailer near Winnemucca
and I looked at my father with his can of Coors

34

listening to the newsman read the tally of death
with his grim jaws working on a piece of steak
and his arms like lobster claws on the TV tray.
And standing there watching him, I suddenly knew
that maybe some of what he told me was just wrong;
that his big boot and ready backhand weren't hotlines to truth.
Like the hotline they kept in a suitcase for the president
to launch the bombs they told us about in school.
And I understood that power didn't make you right.
If it did, all of the powerful would agree on things
but instead the world was matches and gasoline.

So I went outside to kill ants.
I did my best thinking killing ants.
I found a nice bed of them behind our trailer.
I kicked at their main hole, making explosion sounds.
I thought what a disaster this must be in their world
and I imagined little child ants deep in the ground
crawling under their desks and covering their heads,
and a news ant reading them the tally of death.
The little fuckers started running around like crazy.
Standing there watching them
I got an erection.
And that's when I understood the mind of God.
I found an old can of solvent in the shed
and poured it on the ant city and lit it on fire
and I put out the last of the flames with piss
and that was the end of God for me.

blueprint for a night's sleep

Tonight in my bed I won't conjure
the usual cast of oblivion-bringers.
I think that I have moved beyond the reach
of human beings now, tonight.
I will have instead the clean embrace of engines;
my steps will echo like dropped spoons
in a hall of humming turbines
laid in rows like steel corpses
whose transformed electric deeds
course out through buried cables,
into the world, no longer mine.

Once I slept beside a river
and woke up in the night
while a barge was floating by.
I sat up and watched the massive blackness of it,
only deepened by the running lights,
the immense silence of it,
only amplified by a sailor's shout
as it passed me under the stars beyond
the red trace of my father's cigarette
arcing away from the silent darkness that he was
there against the sky.

There's something terrifying about these things we have made
and not only the insane bombs and the killing machines,
the spaceships burning their door-pounding crews,
our furious jealous killer Gods.
But also the small things you can hold in your hand:
the child's doll, the stone idol, the arrowhead
the mortar and the pestle, the obsidian bead;
each a condensed cry
winging out from our tooth-lined hearts.

But there's something safe and enclosing about them too
something hard and cool, relentlessly predictable,
something honest without need of pointless speech,
something father-like.

I was wondering why the old man had appeared to me here
and now I know.
On a night like this, when the human world has broken down,
after a day that has left me numb as a pile of bricks
knowing that I'll wake up in ten years
with the jaws of a steel trap closing on my heart
and not even know why,
who better for a guide
than that journeyman of silence, my father?
For silence is a thing we build, one of our machines,
powered by the turbines of old hurts
and words that never found their way.

I remember now one winter day
lying under a cold green scab of canvas
in the back of his pickup truck,
my mother beside him in the cab
each of them building a silence.

And I laid down on the heap of our belongings
and covered my face,
and drifted off
to the whine of the engine beneath me.

I don't recall a better sleep in this life, old man.

Maybe you could take me home again tonight.

faith – of a kind
(for Elizabeth)

For a thousand years they used to think
you could predict the future
by looking at sheep

guts.

It seems arrogant of me, now, to suppose
that those ancient and serious and righteous folk
who walked this earth so long ago
were entirely wrong.
And I would like to know
what surprises my tomorrows hold.

My compass, however, is pointing away
from murdering a sheep today
though, I do have this strange premonition
that tonight's supper will include

lamb chops.

northern heart
(to Lena, my daughter)

The problem with us is
we're too much alike.

Your newborn angry face was your grandfather looking back at me.
You need to know that he bequeathed us both his wild northern heart
and that I've learned a bit about its care and feeding.

Do not delude yourself that it is vastly true and loving.
It's average in those ways, to tell the truth.
Like all hearts, it wants what it wants,
and there is a price in denying it
as there is a price in following it.

The thing about our heart is: it's a heart made for famine.
It needs long killing winters when the flesh melts away.
It needs paltry meals of saltfish in the months-long darkness.
It needs to stand on heaving decks with icicles in its hair
on desperate voyages where life balances on an axe blade.

It is a heart to see you through, a survivor's heart.
It needs a diet rich in risk to keep it lean and beating strong.
You will be told and told again to take the safe, same path
by those who want you merely to function,
but they do not understand.
Too much summer will slowly kill us.

You will go off and fall in love someday
and I hope you find your fill of summer,
but even if we are separated by a thousand miles
we will always share this savage northern heart,
and we will wake sometimes at the same moment
when a cold wind pushes at our windows.
We will feel our skin begin to loosen on our bones
and our shared northern heart will stir

39

like the head of some beast in its cave
knowing that our new time of hunger
is here.

god enters a poetry contest
(and wins first prize)

I think it's pretty cool being God, although
I don't know what to compare it to.

It's a lot of work, I'll tell you that.

Ah, who am I shitting.
I'm fucking omnipotent.
It's no work at all.

It's autumn now, in the USA,
which is where I hang out most.

The seasons are the result
of my bitch-slapping the world
one night when I was in a rage.

It's a crooked world now
and it always will be,
but what the fuck.

It's resulted in a lot of good poetry,
and this is a beautiful time of year -
but not because of the turning leaves.

Human beings are also turning.

Look at that fellow there,
so drunk that he just hit his head
trying to climb under that bridge
for some warmth absorbed from the day.
He has squandered my gift of Free Will
and therefore he must pay.

But I will dwell with him now.

Look at the blood running
like the shadow of a fist
opening into black fingers.

Look at the moonlight dancing,
like a strung-out stripper, in the blood.

That light contains me.

People love autumn because
it's the time when the leaves begin to die
and they turn such brilliant colors
as they stiffen and fall into stillness.

Well.

I witness the death of everything;
I can see into the quantum mist
between your very atoms.

You spastic bit of convulsing zero.
Think how lovely it is to me

when you die.

lines on being yourself

"Just be yourself," people always say.

Fuck that.

Being myself is a curse;

a dead chihuahua around my neck leaking liquid shit
a cast iron corn cob drilled into my ass
a testicle exploding like an angry boil
a wristwatch with lips shouting that I suck
a tiny army of survivalists doing war games on my balls.

I'm so fucking tired of "me".

I'd rather be *that* man;

No, not the one with the money,
not the one with the prehensile dick,
not the one under a clear pool of formaldehyde love,
nor the one saluting his imaginary jailer,
not the one repairing the mechanical cocksucker.
And no, not the man on a short leash of braided vagina hair.

But that guy-

the guy with the incurable disease
of loving himself
in spite of all the evidence.

invocation

When will you take me up again, oh Muse?
I see the lines of intent-eyed obedient heads
moving like corpuscles in throbbing concrete veins.
So how about a poem, you dumb cunt?

Do I have to stand here all day
flapping my arms in my stinky plaid coat
to get your attention?
Oh, don't flatter yourself,
I've given up on going steady.

I don't even want to feel your tits anymore.
It's just that I have this feeling
like I'm a witness to a very bad accident.
There's jagged metal everywhere
and all these lives are scattered
in little glass cubes on the pavement.
I think that's somebody's arm lying over there,
but I wouldn't give that fat dude mouth-to-mouth
even if I knew him
though I'll gladly speak a poem into his bleeding ear
with the blue and red lights flashing on my face
while his mouth works like some landed fish.

I'm already thinking of how I'm going to end this poem
without folks thinking I'm a major fuckhead.
But, I've got to tell you, it ain't looking good.
So how about a little help,
you stone cold bitch?

Tell me why I've got this dude
walking through the streets of my brain
with a writhing fetus looking out of his armpit.
Tell me why the largest building in my pretend city
has a sphincter for a door.

44

I need to know these things, I'm responsible.
Why does an animate mop with pencil-eraser tits
wait for me on the eleventh floor?
I have to make sense out of all this,
you double-dealing, monkey-assed whore.
But I've got nothing, nothing-
a PH-fucking-D in nothing.
I'm the world's leading expert in nothing
so I can tell you:
nothing has no color.
Nothing will not listen to your reasons
Nothing is what comes out of a zero when it hatches,
and it has absolutely nothing to tell you.

i saw that god of yours

I saw that God of yours the other day,
at least I think it was him.
He didn't act glad to see me,
wouldn't look me in the eye
in line at the hospital cafeteria.
With his blood-stained scrubs,
a little carton of milk on his tray,
and a stale Cobb salad
actin all surly and shit.

Another botched operation.
No doubt showing off.
Giving the man at the next table
some big-time Vegas show
out-of-body-experience.
Instead of watching the knife in that little boy.
Funny how folks talk so much
about near death experiences,
when clearly his best work
is the all-the-way kind.

I saw that God of yours the other day,
climbing out of a raped vagina
with a fetus on a dog leash
like some kind of prized poodle.
He had a stylish coat and hat
and he walked right down the street
just like he owned the world.

Someone asked him for directions,
and he stopped and looked at her
with those crazy barn-owl eyes.
"I can't help you, ma'am," he said.
"I'm just a tourist here, same as you."

I saw that God of yours the other day,
playing the Big Man, buying rounds at the bar,
about three-quarters shit-faced,
bending my ear.
He said, "what y'all don't get is
that this was a *starter* universe.
I was right out of God School...
didn't know shit.
I've had three others since then.
You should see my new one,
so pretty I get hard
just thinking about it.
Got a million-year hard-on,
swear to Me!
But this'n here, I ain't so proud of,
though I can't seem to get shed of it;
I keep coming back.
I guess the first one's always special.
Plus Mary was such a babe
(what? You bought that virgin shit?)
And I just keep thinking I'll see the trick,
find the key to your me-damned fucked-up-ness.
Make it all make sense, like I done it on purpose.
It ain't looking good though, I have to say.
And anyway you're stuck with me, folks.
Remember, I'm a jealous motherfucker.
Ain't no breakin' up with me, nope-
if I can't fuck you, nobody can."

And he leaned on his stool
and farted.
And it stank like

hell.

lines obtained in my front yard in september

The black cat rests beneath the autumn roses
and I think about walking in a crooked line forever;
my memories would fly off like winter sparrows;
my name would become a meaningless croak.

Oh you, my insatiable eater of stillborn words,
dark lady of the branch-obscured high window,
of autumn nights spent looking up from truck beds,
lovely silent freak - forgive me the crime of making you.

Not that I had a choice in it; not that anyone does.
we all need our interior effigies to burn;
we all need a room in us where a lover waits,
but I have stayed away from the world too long.

So let me be a pilgrim now starting from this day.
Let me speak only gibberish in a dead god's tongue.
Let me walk around the crooked world seven times.
Let me find the black stone of sorrow and kiss it.

please

Please direct your attention to the screen in front of you.

Please pass your paper to the student behind you.

Please do not tattoo a mask of rage on your cellmate with ink from a ballpoint pen.

Please keep your hands to yourself.

Please keep your bullets to yourself.

Please keep your tears, anguish, loneliness, despair, confusion, fragments of the sandwich you are eating, shit molecules, ill-chosen cologne, digestive noises, and opinions all to yourself.

Please keep to the right except when passing.

Please do not regard me with contempt as you pass, for I am running as fast I can.

Please keep me in a jar with holes punched in the lid, and a few pieces of stale lettuce.

Please do not pet me - I am a wild creature.

Please allow me to introduce myself.

Please allow me to please you.

Please do not kill me in my sleep with a chef's knife from my own immaculate kitchen.

Please do not feed me; my keepers provide a healthy and adequate diet.

Please do not tap on the glass of my enclosure.

Please do not point to my engorged sex organs and laugh. That would be immature.

Please stay behind the rope barrier.

Please dress and behave appropriately at all times.

Please comply with all corporate policies.

Please do not bring the meeting to order using your penis as a gavel.

Please do not wake in the night and plead with your imaginary deity.

Please do not ask for a second helping of Jesus. We did not prepare enough.

Please excuse my blank stare. It is a symptom of my post-traumatic boredom disorder.

Please keep your arms and legs in the ride at all times.

Please excuse my habit of saying, "okey-dokey, artichokey ". It's either that, or I kill you.

Please, baby, please!

Please do not leave your child unattended. He's a fucking little brat.

Please talk quietly amongst yourselves while we determine what went wrong.

Please direct your attention only to the things that are not currently wrong.

Please wait your turn, even if it never comes.

Please do not suddenly go into the fetal position under your desk.

Please use only your peripheral vision to examine your coworker's cleavage.

Please include a self-addressed, stamped envelope.

Please allow seven to ten days for delivery.

Please do not roll your head down the busy sidewalk like a bowling ball.

Please do not decide that it wasn't worth it, after all.

my life as a hostile nation

I am a secret agent for the country in my head.
I am also its President and Secretary of State.
It's armed forces consist of only myself.
I am the solitary citizen of The United States of Me.
I have to do all the jobs; which, thank you,
is especially hard since there's a war on.
Yes, I declared war on The Shit Out There long ago.
I could endure the encroachment of reality no longer.
I convened an inner committee and declared my independence;
It was very patriotic of me.

It is a fully fledged world war, this war of mine;
Me versus the world.
so far it's a stalemate.
There have been some nasty wounds
within my ranks, it is true.
But so far no fatalities.
I have, to this point,
killed approximately zero of the enemy,
and that number does not appear to be increasing.
The truth is, the military of The United States of Me
isn't very threatening.
The citizens of Me
don't make good soldiers.
They won't follow orders, for one thing.
And they have no respect for authority.
No discipline.

There are rumors down at headquarters that
The Shit Out There doesn't even know
that I'm at war with it.
If you can imagine!
Oh, I do take a prisoner now and then.
Or, perhaps, they take me.
I'm never clear about that.

I put them in a muddy place and give them shoes with holes.
I provide them scant, unappetizing meals on tin plates.
I blare propaganda at them 24/7 through huge loudspeakers.
I subject them to surprise inspections.
I shout loudly into their faces in my foreign tongue.
They assume that this is my clumsy way
of making love to them.
Fools.
They know nothing of the exigencies of war.
In the end, they always escape.
Or I do.
And I am alone again, out on patrol.

I spend much of my time
in my role as 'secret agent';
a clandestine operative of the Me Republic
deep, deep behind enemy lines.
I have learned to take on the appearance
and behavior of the opposing forces.
I move freely among them,
performing my assigned function,
exactly as though I were one of them.
I have adopted a loose-jowled, semi-smile
that they find very reassuring.
I have become a 'hale fellow well met';
a 'good guy'; 'one of the gang'.
"Good morning!" I call out with my loose jowls.
"Working hard, or hardly working?" I inquire.
"I see you got the 'blue shirt' memo!" I jest.

I live and work among them as one of their own,
a valued member of their boot-licking ranks.
They do not suspect my deep subterfuge;
that, far from being one of them,
I am a hostile nation of one in their very midst
working unstintingly toward their annihilation.

I have gathered much intelligence over the years.
I have become expert in the ways of my enemy.
As I move among them with my sagging face,
at times I wonder if anything of my true identity remains,
I have become so adept at assuming a false aspect.
And it's true that the task of winning this war
seems quite overwhelming at times;
when you consider it dispassionately
the odds seem impossibly against me.
And sometimes I long for an ally in my struggle,
some friendly nation with whom a pact might be struck,
A concordance hammered out.
But such a thing would be a betrayal,
a cowardly treason to the nation of myself.

There is a park near my work
where I often eat a sandwich;
and there is a place in this park
where two trees come out of the ground.
Their trunks are smooth and flesh-like
and only a little larger than human thighs.
They make me think of the legs of a giant;
buried head-down in the soil,
plunged into the earth by the fist of some angry god.
I sit and rest from the labor of passing unnoticed,
and I think of the buried giant beneath me.
I visualize his beautiful warrior's body,
now becoming one with clod and stone.
His arms reaching out in a frozen flail,
splayed fingers dwindling into dark tendrils,
his penis a magnificent taproot,
drilling down down into the black earth.

I sit there at noontime on hot summer days
having long talks with my subterranean brother,
for I understand that he is buried

only in a trivial physical sense.
In other realms he moves
with the speed of a rampaging killer,
the agility of a hunting predator,
and we regale each other
with tales of our respective wars.
His in the land of myth and stone,
mine here among these human insects;
and it is a solace to us both, I think.

Afterward I will sometimes sit in silence
sensing the heat of his trapped fury beneath me
and these are the moments when
my loneliness briefly abates, but
there must always come the time
when I rise and brush off my hands
and walk away. And know
that I am really the buried fighter;
I am the one who is
turning into stone.

son of pool cue

A piece of past captured
in wet throbbing meat:
the memory of words
from someone reminiscing
about biker chick rage
(yes, breasts and butt flash,
clad in... denim, not leather)
expressed via pool cue into
last-call vagina.

A savage world, this,
and I didn't make it.

But I am largely built of this stuff;
memories of memories,
a spaghetti bowl of stories,
comprehensible only to
idiot bastard lunatics
in a junkyard of abandoned hearts.
And don't point your Buddha at me.
That 'no self' shit is deader than
a streetful of burnt monk ashes.

Poems do not, in general, write themselves.
These words, in this order, are evidence of
something.
But to therefore speak of 'truth' therein,
is to dine on the haunches of road kill unicorns
run down by the vehicle of your assumptions
on a highway in the state of confusion.

Tales of savagery, of longing and lust,
of finding
and of losing,
of living and of ceasing to live,

some tossed into me by passersby;
like the one about the biker chick
dealing with a lesbian advance
late one night
on the wrong side of some town.

Let this poem be the squalling infant
resulting from that dark copulation.
Let these words shine the light of awareness
into that bloody vagina,
and let this conglomeration
of pixelated characters
be a strictly bring-your-own-judgment party.
And I will greet you at the door and tell you:

"Welcome to this poem.

Welcome to me."

the problem with poems

The problem with poems is that you can't live in them.
Oh, you can stay for a while and the truth will get on top
and fuck you like a porn star while you smoke a cigar.
And the world will fit together like fine handmade carpentry,
but sooner or later you go out blinking like a mole rat,
into the autistic boy's face on the 603 bus;
with caramel sperm harvested from politicians in sex scandals
seeping through the ceiling with a slow, sad drip.

The problem with poems is that you can't spend them.
I put one under a dancer's g-string in Tulsa.
And the fat snuff-chewing lesbian bouncer
got her baseball bat out from under the bar,
so I walked out and gave one to a panhandler
who transformed into a feral, rabid, oil company CEO
in a very expensive suit
encrusted with vomit
humping my leg like a libidinous mongrel.

The problem with poems, is that they just don't love you.
You can lavish them with hours of attention and care
fondle them like the pale breasts of a wall street mistress.
You can whisper soft sexy praise with your tongue a tweaking slug,
but they don't care. They'll just look at you
with eyes like the wounds on a prison yard corpse
and go off with the first sad trembling fuck that comes by
leaving you so alone it feels like you're falling forever.

The problem with poems is that people won't hear them.
We've been traumatized by numb hours in English class,
studying the pissing contests of corporate whore intellectuals
and useless insights from the merry jaunts of smug fucks,
who've sucked enough professor dick to live near the woods.
We've been served up the sour menses of obscure southern twats
while fist-faced cops with guns walk the halls leaving fart trails.

Poems should be the just, rageful roar of the masses
but instead they're just another way to come up short.

The problem with poems is that they leave you stranded.
Oh, they'll look at you with glistening eyes in the barroom light
of some deep hidden place in your heart's bone city.
And for a while your tongue is a cold crystal tool
digging with blaze into the wet membranes of reality,
and you can see it all hanging right there in the air
like mathematical proof, a chemical equation.
But when you try to tell it,
your voice is the empty wind
blowing over the all the sad sagging heads in cubicles,
on it's way to oblivion-
disturbing nothing.

Take These Words
(a groovy pop song)

(To be performed by a middle-aged man screaming through a cheap cardboard megaphone, accompanied by hard rock guitars, drums, etc, and two awesome go-go dancers in bikinis, one on either side.)

Take these words as my soundtrack to every stress induced facial twitch occurring exactly now in a hundred million cubicles.

Take these words to hover about you like angry black bees as you bed down in the damp grass by the river of your delusion.

Take these words under your long stained coat and discreetly feed them table scraps in a diner at 2:00 AM in the bone city.

Take these words to stand lookout as you slake your dark need in the blind alley, bathed in silver light from a pitiless moon.

Take these words so you can say them when you come home to find the famous CEO wiping his ass on your best towels.

(sax solo...)

Take these words that will scuttle off like sandcrabs at the first sign of your hidden anguish when you fall to your mortgaged steel knees.

Take these words to greedily drink your tears as you sit with the blooming hurt of your wrongdoing though you could have done no other.

Take these words to conclude your epic life with choking on a cocktail olive while discussing dog breeds with a former porn actress.

Take these words that I have gathered like armfuls of stillborn fetuses resulting from the rapes of a conquering army existing only in rumors.

Take these words for $69.95 as a frugal alternative to human love as they endure your desperate advances with unblinking eyes.

Take these words they are all I have for you now after going to and fro in the world and walking up and down in it.

Take these words I think they mean something; they are burning holes in the floors of my lungs and my throat and my head and

59

the light is shooting out like a million lightspeed needles.
Take these words. Take these words. Take these words.

(repeat and fade...)

trouble

I have never courted trouble
but trouble finds me.
Like a bounty hunter it tracks me down
drags me wailing into the night
duct tapes my snarling mouth
and throws me hogtied into its trunk.
It drives me back, back,
back to the bone city.
And during the long hours in my steel cocoon
tires whining beneath me,
I shit and piss myself like a swaddled infant,
but I have time to think:

and I see where I went wrong!

To avoid trouble you must embrace it.
Take it into your mouth like a wad of sour flesh
let it fuck you in the ass;
play dead and give it everything so it will
slap your limp carcass with a disinterested paw
and skulk away to find some other fool.

Ablaze with new insight my fists ring out.
I pound on my trunk and trouble hears me-
stops and hauls me out like shit-filled luggage
rips the tape from my mouth and snakes its savage tongue
like hot cable down into my raw aching throat.
We both know that now
I am trouble's willing bitch.

But in knowing this I am free!

I lope through the bone city with pile-driver legs.
Bam! Bam! Bam!
Each stride is half a block.

Buildings rattle
Windows break
bone infants wail bonily as
their skeleton moms scoop them up.

And my words- my words!

My mouth is now a Gatling gun
spewing forth words like bullets.
Each line of my poem
clears a sidewalk of bone ones,
and I lob stanzas into the skeleton crowd
like deadly grenades of meaning.
And the bone people clatter
and fall apart in heaps; becoming
the archeology of this minute.
For now in their dry silence-
their story will be told.

But I am tired now
and I am out of bullets.
And though I am unconsumed
(I am yet a flesh and blood human being)
I am as alone as ever.
And I hear bone sirens,
and I know they are for me.
And up the bone-littered street
I see trouble driving up
in his big black sedan.

notes on suburban living

I dreamed I was swallowed by an enormous eel made of cross-eyed
   George Washington heads.

Does this explain why my neighbors squint through narrow curtain
   gaps?

Advice for the unemployed suburbanite: with a little stealth one could
   easily subsist on the nutritious flesh of neighborhood pets.

My neighbors do not suspect that I roam the streets at night, my face
   a mask of hunger.

To take a leisurely walk in the suburbs is to feel a sniper taking distant
   aim at your affable face.

Watching the neighborhood children trundle to school, I reflect that
   they are condensed clots of their parents' misdirected rage.

My head comes apart in sections like a peeled orange.

Unable to see each others' penises, we suburban men judge lawns
   instead.

Our deepest fear is that our wives will take up with lawn-care rene-
   gades.

Occasionally one of us goes mad and is found naked, huddled fearful-
   ly in a hedge.

When a neighbor allows his dog to shit on my lawn, I collect it and
   mail it back to him with an anonymous note enclosed. Our laws
   must be enforced.

I furtively glance at my neighbor's wife's vagina which belches a hot
   bubble of mucous.

This is a working class suburb; each pickup truck gleams like a sad
   apparition in the light of an acid moon.

Each of us keeps a private arsenal in hopes of a time of chaos that will
   extricate us from our grinding lives.

The cats are actually in charge, judging from their expressions.

The police spend hours waiting in their cars, wishing one of us would
   freak out.

The geometry of the suburb suggests that each family must be enclosed and given ample space, much like hazardous waste.

All of the portraits of jesus get together and gossip shamelessly each night.

what dead elvis never said to mama cass
(in a swanky vegas suite)

I ain't calling you mama,
you ain't my mama.

You the mama of a litter of 50,000 dead puppies
their cold purple leather lips still stuck to you
in a cardboard box under Eddie Haskell's bed.

You the mama of a generation of headless chickens
murdered by rumors of satan-worshiping day care owners.

You the mama of Bill's test tube bastard
from the stuff off that blue dress-

You the mama of Obama.

You the mama of an infant predator drone
with autism and a cleft palate
and a beating heart,
on the outside of its steel body.

You Bill Gate's mama.

You the mama of a fetus exactly like Karl Rove
only smaller and smarter and meaner.

You the mama of Jim Beam, Jack Daniels,
a gym bag full of loaded guns,
and every stripper with a Walmart breast job.

You everybody's mama, baby.
And I'm their papa.
But you ain't my mama
and it's show time here in bone Vegas-

so come on back to bed.

kim and me and barns in imaginary oklahoma

It's the old barns we want to see
as we drive through Oklahoma,
The sun beating down on my left arm,
the hot air whipping around us
looking at your knees up against the dashboard,
and down those honey thighs.
It's the barns with Jesus Saves painted on them
or Dentures $99.

When we stop for gas I look at people's teeth.
They are indeed strangely large and white,
piano keys in gray faces.
I worry we'll be devoured by $99 chompers.
We do not belong here, after all.
You are far too beautiful
and I have small, rat-like teeth.

We drive on, passing barn after barn
the best ones bleached gray
the roofs dented in-
and you think about standing there
in the middle of some night that never happened
in a silence so deep it sings in your ears;
just you and your regrets
singing to you.

Fifty miles from Amarillo the sun goes down.
Nothing out there looks saved to me.
As darkness comes on we have nothing to say.
We're tired of this dead land hurtling by
but the barns keep passing us in the night,
the most beautiful abandoned long ago,
on the edge of being nothing now
just like you and me.

Part 3

correct emotions III

I always think
about how you came out
purple like a writhing prune
tiny flailing arms and legs.
The cord like a black tarred rope
glistening around your neck.
I understood with my body (not my mind)
that you were literally one minute from death.

I ran beside the little wheeled table,
down the dim 3:00 AM hospital hall,
to a room with machines and tubes
where they sucked your first black shit
out of your tiny tortured windpipe
and you bloomed, son.

I saw you bloom
from the color of somebody's black eye
all the way to a wonderful life-infused pink.
In ten fucking enormous heart-crushing seconds
the oxygen spilled into your shiny new blood
and you cried out mad as all outrageous hell
at this searing bright world in which you found yourself.

You never knew it but something bloomed in me too.
Something else was born while I stood there watching;
that plugged me into this world's absurd electric jaws,
chewing on my outlaw heart through all the viscous hours.
I carried you with me
down a thousand gauntlets of false smiles.
You lived in my pocket while the serrated rows of blank faces,
sliced daily through the braided arteries of my essence.
I pressed your nighttime cries into the pages of my life;
now a bleached-out history I wear like a jailhouse t-shirt;
but there are no regrets, far from it.

I'd do it all again the same.
I'd do it the same for each pebble God drops into his sheepskin bag
to tally all the births and the lives and the deaths for now and ever.
But let there be no correct emotions between us: you're a piece of me.
You're my arm and my guts and my voice and my heart.
So I'll tell it to you straight:
do not listen to those who would spill you
like precious water on the corrosive sands of their inner deadness.
Do not take the bargain offered by the twitching sweaty face of your
    own fear.
Keep this poem that I am making for you
as a talisman against the shadows;
Where carrion tongues of delusion fuck your ear
and dark winds whisper death words
and you are lost and shunned and hunted,
as I have carried you,
I ask you now to carry me.

what this bartender in clearfield, utah would say
(if he could)

So maybe I'll reach out and take it
while you're looking into my eyes.
Not that I want it,
no.
I want something-
not sure what yet.
Look at my eyes-
keep looking.
See how I'm smiling a little?
That don't mean shit.
I ain't thinking nothing.
That's bad grammar;
some people go around
correcting grammar.
I don't cotton to that
I don't take kindly.
I'm fixin to take my belt sander
to your high falutin nuts
because I am a hillbilly,
yes.
And fuckit I'm proud.
Lemme tell ya story
bout a man
flitting behind the dark bushes.
(Nobody saw me)
I'm going to try to forget it now.
If I was that bad, I wouldn't feel guilty
right?
But you're not lookin in my eyes.
My eyes
look into my eyes.
You say you have to choose which?
Can't look into both at once?

Yeah... I've been there.
I suggest you look into the right eye-
No,
the one on YOUR right.
That's it,
look deeply within
like going down a long tunnel
into the subterranean city of my soul.
The streets are empty
except for a few homeless crazies.
And that man there,
see him dodge behind that bush,
that steel bush of rusted sticks.
Because nothing grows here
in the buried city of my soul,
everything is concrete:
steel
brick

dead.

lines to a dancer

Breath in strobe-flash stuttering.
Movement of full embedded flesh.
Proximity of head, cheek, delicate chin,
recognition of dried sweat on veined skin.
I run a mental hand up those slim smooth hips and watch
skull pasties ride flawless mounds as you bend
back back back on the brass bar.

Soon I'll walk out of here and see the sun going down
through the needles of distant light poles
in sad empty fields.
I'll stop for a pack of cigarettes while
some tattooed fool in a wife beater sets
his bitch straight in the parking lot. But
now I'm watching you turn and sway
with that crazy beautiful back, and you
make that awkward dainty move with your hips
that is yours
and yours alone.

I throw my shot down and feel it burn
knowing that your knees are hurting and
your bad tooth is acting up. And
your current old man treats your kids like shit, and
I think of you on some long gone summer night on the
lost planet of your youth.
Playing kick-the-can, breathing fast, and running hard.
Just another neighborhood kid - and I
wish I'd been there with you running
into the vast hot sweaty mysterious night.

lines found at the bottom of an escaped-from box

I will not say that I meant no harm;
there were too many days when fear made me cruel.
I will not say that I spoke the truth;
far too often did I indulge in vain crowing.
I will not say that I erred out of passion;
I've squandered years of my life being empty meat.
I will not say that I was guided by love;
I am still addicted to long talks with the dark one.
I admit my failure in these common things
which any who count themselves good will claim.
I will tell you only this, my friends: I see you
here among the corn chips and football and ass cancer
and in my better moments, I've even seen it doesn't matter
which of us takes the truth out of God's diamond beak.

fifteen

When I was fifteen,
I was in love with a girl.
With an east coast accent
and freckles on her breast
and on her thin pale arms,
which moved so beautifully
when she told me her story.
And the night was as warm
as a mouthful of spit.
I rested my chin
on my bike handlebars
wanting to put words
into the lonely sounds
of trucks on the freeway.
But I could only look up
and watch the distant flame
down at the refinery
flicker and dance,
like a sad burning ghost,
which knew that my longing
would swallow the world.

lines purchased in a coffee shop for $2.49

Her green eyes touch these coffee shop faces.
Like small birds that I watched come to roost
in a tree on a cold morning long ago.
Her caramel cheeks and strong black brows
speak of royal lines in distant dead kingdoms.
I know that she has small hands with damp palms
though I will neither see nor touch them.
And eavesdropping tells me that she has plans
about which she is presently much excited.
I give all her projects my silent blessing,
and I invite her face into this morning's poem, because
its only imperfection is the lack of a mole
near the right corner of her full-lipped mouth.
And because I think I will never answer the question:
Is she more or is she less beautiful for that?

cat with moth wings

Cliff was a human being but narrowed down now into
something like a big, foul-smelling,
needing-a-shave insect that did
nothing but kill shit with a hard, venom-dripping stinger
and stuff it into a hole for future hatchlings to eat. Only
Cliff's role in this particular ecosystem,
here in a sad suburb
a dozen miles from the bone city,
was to turn cheap vodka and bummed cigarettes into
stories about shit that never happened;
and nobody wanted to hear about anyway.
But it would have been bad manners
to stand there saying nothing,
letting the sounds of the bar settle over you
like sediment at the bottom of a sea of tattooed stupid,
to be fossilized and dug up in a million years like some dinosaur.

Cliff lived two blocks from the bar which is good because
he didn't own a car and on this hot summer night we see him
walking back home with a Styrofoam box full of chicken wings think-
    ing,
they better gave me the right fuckin sauce!
Because this is a big investment for Cliff, these wings.
He doesn't often get take-out and he wouldn't have this time except
the grocery store is a half mile away
and by the time he thought about it
he was too liquored up to make the trip.
So he splurged on the wings and planned to
take them home
and eat them
while watching TV.

He was walking there as night came down
in a place that was no place,
in a place with no history,

where nothing was remembered,
and where you wake up in a strange room
in the gray haze of dawn
on a vomit-stained carpet hearing
the breath-fugue of a nest of passed-out strangers.
You wake up trying to remember a dream
but all you have is a glass spike in your heart
and the television is still on selling you spot remover,
or you wake up and drop your feet to the floor
and sit there in the dark with your head in your hands
until you finally understand the arithmetic of getting up.

At first Cliff thought it was just another cat
but it was glowing strangely,
somehow giving off light,
walking out of an adjacent parking lot,
slowly,
accurately,
and even at this distance
in the falling dark he could see
that it was regarding him,
with a look of knowing,
with a look of challenge.

Cliff was at that moment aware
of the stale air under his clothes,
the smell of his unwashed body,
the three days growth on his chin,
and his being three quarters drunk.
That's when the strange animal before him
opened its dusty, multicolor wings.

It was a moment fixed in the amber of time,
such a mystery,
history dripping down like syrup,
recognizing the miracle of this instant.
Mythical beast!

We've always had these
flying like a winged shadow from another world
between the buildings
over the strip malls
through the midnight parking lots.

Cliff stood and looked,
at first with sadness and a kind of guilt,
but slowly a feeling of greed rose up in him.
What will I do? What will I do with it?
One step forward...
but the thing lifted its head, stopping him.

He put down the container of wings.
He saw himself on TV talking
about this cat,
this moth cat,
one of a kind,
unique in the world like Nessy or Sasquatch.
Some goddamn thing.
And the money, the money!
Finally for once in his life
to be the big man at the bar,
buying the drinks.
The owner for once looking at him
not like some piece of dick cheese,
but with respect and with deference.
"Yeah, buy the man a drink.
'Course it's on me.
Here keep the change."

He took a step toward the thing
and it didn't move now.
It was waiting for him,
as though God had torn a hole in the world
and was looking through at him.

Yes, he was afraid the thing would bite him
and even more afraid that it would fly away,
but there was no turning away from this,
no being lazy about this.
This shimmering creature beyond beauty,
beyond wanting.

And a wind came up,
the last wind in the world.
Cliff bent down and reached out his hand,
and at the moment he would have made contact
he found himself falling, falling.
He had fallen into the cat with moth wings,
the hole that God had torn to look at him
He was hurtling in utter blackness
but the thing was still with him
shimmering beside him.
It brought itself closer as he fell
and it kissed him with its needle-toothed feline mouth.
Cliff felt the velvet fur around the lips of God
and the tongues of the two beings;
one God and one Cliff
entwined there in the falling
ripping him down the center of his soul
and he perceived the utter unlikelihood
of the contents of each passing miniscule shard of Now.
The clear viscous jelly we have created to live within
to shield us from the burning acid wind of what is real
and he knew that each instant of life is an instant
spent falling headlong into God.
Not the God of the churches,
not Jesus senior
not some jealous child demanding to be eaten, no!
But the ancient, ancient, ancient idea of God;
the God that is everything OUT THERE
the God that we inhabit like mindless mites,

the God that is the software
running in the multi-cored supercomputer,
that is every single fucking thing with a mind!

Cliff plunged his tongue
like a wafting tubular animal of the deepest sea
like the dick of a rapist,
like the arm of a mewling infant seconds from the cunt;
reaching, delving, cleaving, wanting,
having, killing, fucking, running, coming, exploding...
When cliff came to
he was lying on the sidewalk
next to his box of wings
and he sat up and thought his eyes were maybe lasers
burning holes and slicing swathes
through this bogus fucked-up world
this laughable 'reality'.
And he felt the imperative that every prophet has always felt
coursing through his blood
pounding in his temples
throbbing in his heart:
The imperative to take it forth to the people
to lift up their rheumy, bloodshot eyes
to clean out their shit-stuffed ears
to bring them blinking out of the cave of shadows.

He got to his feet and walked the hundred yards
in the dusky light back to the bar.
He went through the door
and felt the clear warm jelly air of the place
settle over him like it always did.
But he felt it this way for the very first time
and it was all he could do to keep from retching,
so he stood inside the door for a minute
and just looked and listened.

There was Ron-John the bartender

talking to Stu,
his bar towel over his shoulder like always and
Stu's gut burgeoning out over his lap
like always.
Stu was laughing and the other regulars at the bar looked over
and Cliff could see the complex mechanism before him.
A beautiful but sad machine,
with all the parts working
like the inside of a Rolex;
a thing of utter beauty.
He could see now, yes,
and he slowly walked up next to Stu
and put his hands carefully on the bar
and Ron-John looked at him and said,
"What the hell, I thought you left."
"Well, I came back," said Cliff, lamely,
for there was so much to say.
And now he could see how impossible it was;
how there was no sanctioned way to say these things
and maybe that's why they never got said.
But he had to try.
So he looked at Ron-John
and looked at Stu and said,
"Something happened while I was walking home…"
Ron-John said, "Shit, I think he's starting to cry."
Stu said, "Maybe he got ass-raped."
Ron-John said, "No, he'd like that.
Hey, Cliff where's your chicken wings?"
And Stu said, "Cliff, did some mean man ass rape you
and then fuckin take your wings?"

Ron-John and Stu laughed
and the regulars looked over and laughed
while Cliff just stood there trying to smile.
Because he knew that they were laughing
into the hoods over their blind heads

just before the gallows floor dropped away
and the rope snapped tight
and their lives squeezed all sudden into their skulls,
their eyes popping out and swinging
adangle by nerve onto their bloody cheeks.
It was their own slow murder
they were laughing at
but there was no way to tell them.
So he just stood there.
What else could he do?
And then he saw Tyler, the karaoke guy
getting his gear set up on the little stage.
He knew it must be almost nine o'clock
and soon folks in various stages of inebriation
would be singing their guts out
where the measure of success
was to sound exactly like the hit song
that everybody had heard for over thirty years.
to remove as much of themselves as they possibly could
until with luck, there would be nothing left.
That's when folks praise you
because make no mistake:
it isn't easy being nothing
it isn't easy being not there
it isn't easy donning the shroud
and leaving nothing of you behind.

Cliff signed up to be the first singer.
He waited until Tyler called his name
and then he climbed up on the stage.
He took the mic and ignored the music and began to shout:

"People! My...friends?! Don't you know that
the first and biggest joke that they've sold us is time?
As though a second spent with your nuts in a vice
is the same thing as a second spent shooting your wad

into some sexy woman all moaning your name?
As though there is some kind of ruler
they can hold up to your life?
Let me tell you,
according to that clock I've been gone a half hour,
but in orgasm time it's been a whole man's full life.
I went through a hole into another world
and its form was a cat, yes,
a cat with moth wings.
Which it had to be, yes, don't you see?
Because I doesn't make sense.
Because it can't be real.
That's the point.
It was a signpost on the road to heaven
to hell
to nirvana
to a burning lake of truth.
If I could give it to you I would give it to you.
I would grab you like a rag doll
in my trashcan-lid hands.
I would lift you up.
I would shake the knowing into you.
Because I am you.
This ain't some cliche bullshit.
I am the heart you are the lung.
I am the head and you are the hand.
In the same body…"

They had to hold Cliff down
to get the mic away.
He wouldn't stop yelling
so they called the police.

A cop came with handcuffs and took him away.
And if that cop had only turned around as he drove,
he might have saved himself that night.

He might have seen it in time-
The broad cat's head with those bottomless eyes,
gazing at his throat like a hungry god.

lines to a stripper's birthmark on a sunday afternoon

Moving there before me in the dim deceptive light,
near enough to breathe upon yet distant as a moon.
Wine-hued flawless blemish undulating in my sight
remaining indecipherable as some forgotten rune;

Signifying something no one really understands
though it carries all the secrets I will ever need
to live among these blighted souls in this benighted land.
If only that bewitching stain were something I could read.

I look into your eyes in hopes of getting help from you.
But something tells me you are quite as mystified as I
And from your lovely quarter no assistance will ensue
In comprehending this suggestive but elusive sign.

I call, "Another shot here, Carmen. I think I'll have to stay.
The world is far too fucked to view in that piss-yellow sun.
If there be Gods, this mark is part of what they have to say.
Who am I to leave before the scripture lesson's done?"

lines appearing in the mirror while shaving

The point about a razor's edge is that
it's hard to balance on. But
my razor is a six lane highway and
the problem isn't balancing it's
dodging traffic or
waking up at 4 am thinking: I'll
find the answer,
pick the lock,
break the code,
fifty-three years old and
still thinking there's a trick,
a loophole.
Still trying to fuck a padlock with my
middle-aged dick and
yes, I do plan to live to 106
fuck you very much.

to the six directions

I am told

that people who once lived here
invoked the six directions.

I am told

that if I dig in this ground
I will find the shards of their pots.
I will find the fragments of their weapons.
I will find tubers grown of their blood.
I will find clay envelopes enclosing their bones.

But there is asphalt here now,
and the wind carries no coyote's voice.
It carries only the cries of diesel engines
and we no longer dance
where wolves pace nervously
at the firelight's edge.

Our voices have been stolen
and stored outside our bodies
to be sold back to us,
like street junky plasma
to staunch our inner wounds.

If we ape the dead rites
of these ancient murdered;
it is a joke,
an obscenity,
an utterance more profane
than any possible curse.
For our spirit-world contains only
the ghosts of middle-managers
checking their flies in elevators;

our shamans have MBA's,
and clogged arteries,
and acid reflux,
and the sour stench of constant fear
under their crisp, slave-made shirts.
And they tell us about nothing but spreadsheets.

But I am here in this place
and I am yet a human being.
And I have need for an intervention
with unseen forces.

When I look at this ground sideways,
I see a village of stone faces
like drowned bodies
under a placid asphalt pond.
I see that each handful of dirt
is only the dried mingled blood
of ten thousand nameless dead ones.
And I feel the yearning of this ground
to have it's savage history declaimed,
I feel the yearning of the dead ones
to be remembered.
I feel the imperative of singing the song
of this place and this moment and this body.
So I will ring out my own salutation,
with no dimestore rattle nor plastic beads nor flute
carved by some failed accountant in a tie-dyed shirt;
but with my own honest voice,
singing what it sees and what it knows.

To the East:
Wellspring of decisions and relentless machines,
of whispered rumors of impossible cities,
of ridge-line riders in the cold light of morning,
of mysterious disease and murderous Gods, and the
hatched-faced woman with her hungry-eyed brood

of days that slice history into before and after
patron spirit of embarkation.
Source of new days and fresh starts;
of decisions and change and striking out,
faithful attendant of all first fucks,
smiling goddess of the morning erection.

To the West:
Badlands- place of night and the outlaw
refuge of ghosts and haunted lost souls.
Where the hunted repair to heal their wounds,
and the shiny car slams into John Wayne Manson,
and the driver leaves the scene on foot.
Under nervous bright cones of helicopter searchlights
where the lonesome hippie bathes in the outgoing surf
proffering his collectivist dream to the sea;
While his children sell insurance to drunk businessmen in bars
and the names of his whore daughter's stillborn children
hang in the air like a poisonous mist.

To the North:
Source of cold winds and the bureaucrat's blank stare
of the dreamless sleep and the buried dormant seed.
Land of shadow and retraction,
where bad memories lie frozen under a mile of ice.
Source of the hardened heart and folded arms
where the dead god waits on a slab for his autopsy.
Where emotions are put away for now
so that crucial business can be conducted.
Spirit of stolid guards, motionless at the palace gate.
Friend of the policeman now approaching your window
place of just not answering anymore.

To the South:
Where the hot mud swallows the fugitive's feet
and the warm river flows into the infinite sea.
Land of longing and reaching and embracing

of the moments when letters are dropped into slots.
Source of jealousy and greed and suicide
and the lawless arithmetic of pure desire,
of snipers taking aim in distant high towers
where the off-center mouth contorts in the dark,
waiting with a knife for its faithless lover.
Where all is forgotten and all is forgiven
and the soul is returned like a borrowed book.

To the Sky:
Place of burning light and the ruthless true vision.
Home of justice and clear sight and penetration
of the chiseled stone face with ball-bearing eyes.
Source of God-charged lightning piercing your brain
where the dark bloody lake reflects the light of fireworks
while the boy king is murdered in his innermost chamber.
Place of destructive creation and creative destruction
from whence the horny God descends to his mortal lover.
Wellspring of all prophets and rebels,
of the relentless machinery of the lovely idea,
of the moment you realize what it is that you've done.

To the Earth:
Mother, womb and tomb, place of birth and decay,
from which all is spawned and to which all returns.
Where the seed uncurls and the blind worm moves
and the predator's body powers ancient trees.
Where the eyes of cadavers stare silently upward
and the loaded spider waits in stillness for a meal.
Place of renewal and growth and transformation
and the embarrassing fact of our ultimate unity
stored in the greedy fists of dirt-clinging roots.
Where the badger encircles her nursing litter
while the stone woman's nipple dissolves in the rain.

And so let it be thus known and understood;
that I did not pass this place unaware,

that I recognized the village of asphalt faces,
that I welcomed them into the rooms of my voice,
and that I carry them with me as I walk these streets.
Let the spirits that I have summoned attend me now
on my tiny sea journeys on desolate mornings.
Between the texture islands on my dawn-lit ceiling
and as I turn on some corner into the pulsing throng
like ancient water pouring into the river of life.

thinking of someone

I am sending out a vagrant piece of longing now,
to steal into the back door of your boarded-up heart.
To make friends in there with your crazy cat,
snoop in the refrigerator for a midnight snack
and then make himself a cup of tea and sit,
For there is no hurry now in this;
There is no hurry now.

He knows that you sleep in a room upstairs;
he will await your call with the utter patience
of one who has captured all his future days
like grains in this salt-bowl on your simple table.
And with them seasons his meal of life.
And with them seasons his meal of death.

As you lie above him his thoughts will dwell
upon the dark terrain of your sleeping body.
He will walk the soft ridge of a flawless thigh
and camp by the sweet swell of your breath-moved belly.
A grinning coyote will climb the rise of one breast
and call out laughing at the lovely joke of it.

He will have visitors, of course, coming out of the walls
Who will argue the merits of dead politicians,
discuss fictional weather in unwritten novels,
and then stand at the window with their 'O'-shaped mouths
And hang there, looking out, waiting, waiting.
And my longing will stand among them for a time,
for he is a gentle thing, and they are so sad.

But when all your ghosts have come away from the window
and have settled down like old clothes in their attic trunks.
He will put down his tea and he will climb the stairs.
And the cat will lift its head and show it's crazy green eyes

as he slips into bed with the you at the exact center of you,
and softly caresses that beautiful sleeper.

a toast for julieann

Gathered here in wine-drenched huddle, once again conspiring
on a world in slomo suicide with sitcom laugh track.
I would ask a second to my motion that all below be well and roundly
    fucked.
As we four look down like pale-fleshed Greek Gods in a bad B movie,
and our diamond words, falling, transform into cruel-eyed harpies,
strafing with their pitiless sight all who do not own their freight of
    genius.

Part 4

correct emotions IV

This poem is for all the unsung heroes throughout history.
The little people like you and me that you never hear about,
but who quietly commit small acts of heroism each day.
Like the patriot who was never late for his job of gassing Jews.
And the plantation overseer who whipped only with reluctance.
To all gang-raping racist bikers who beat up faggots,
I see you there riding for 'Bikers Against Child Abuse'!
To all those believers who pray sincerely for guidance,
but then a psycho killer God promises seventy virgins,
I welcome you to my poem (but that's a shitload of virgins).
To that CIA technical writer updating the torture manual,
who scrupulously resists stealing office supplies each day,
I know this isn't much of a poem but it's partly for you.
To the guy who selflessly works overtime writing software
to allow a single guard to monitor dozens of prisoners,
your computer code will witness the insanity of thousands.
Welcome to this, poem, dude. Grab a beer and sit down.
To the new-age bookshop owner spying on her employees
through her iphone while lying on a beach on vacation,
This poem thanks you for your commitment to our awakening.
To the drone operator at his console in the suburbs of my city,
who worries that the human being he just snuffed was quite small for
    a man.
I'm keeping a place next to me on the couch for you, buddy.
Oh, and leave room for me: the fool writing poetry no one reads,
who squanders his days in the intestines of the beast,
sucking his sustenance out of the passing shitstream.
For all my snarling words I belong here most of all.
So let this poem be a refuge for the morally mediocre;
for those of us who could have been a helluva lot worse.
The flag saluters, church attenders, holders of doors open,
feelers of correct emotions, doers of The Right Thing.
We imagine chambers deep in distant steel mountains
where those who plan the world work furiously away.

But we are not those people, we do not make the plan.
And now we're coming to the end and we're all here,
each of us naked, rat-sized, writhing in a single mass.
And a beautiful body swims in the vast lake of us.
We each take a bite with our tiny pinched faces.
She is all there is and she will not reach the shore.

the button

It is important to work well as part of a team.
Your teammates are depending on you.
You are in high school now.
It's the night of the Big Game.
The crowd is like a single roiling body
And the cheerleaders are so pretty
it makes you a little sad.
The air is crisp with cold and excitement,
and then suddenly one of the team of Us is injured
by the team of Them.
By all the accounts you are permitted to hear,
that hit was against The Rules.
A dirty trick.
It is important, as a team, to respect The Rules.
It is well known, however, that They do not.
Respect the rules.
Because They are different from Us.
And now a boy lies twitching on the ground.
You want him to just shake it off.
That's what we nearly always do.
We don't want to let the team down.
But he is not getting up.
They are taking him away.
He will be all right.
Don't worry about him.
Walk through this door.
It is time to be an adult.
This is where you will sit.
In a few years, if things go well,
you will sit over there.
Time for lunch! Let's go eat!
This is your city.
It is a wilderness, in a sense,
Except that everything is owned.

Everything is property.
You would learn this if you were one of Them
with no money,
and needed to use the bathroom.
But you're one of Us, so no worries about that!
Enjoy your nice lunch.
It's so good, and so much!
Think about those less fortunate.
They are somewhere, but not here.
You should pause to be grateful.
To be one of Us.
Good news!
You've exceeded expectations!
We're letting you hold the button!
The button is cutting-edge.
The button is state-of-the-art.
The button is smooth and flawless
like a cheerleader's breast.
Look! Do you see that man there?
He is planning to hurt us.
Quick! Push the button!
You think he might hate us
because of the button?
That thinking is not useful to the team.
It will not bring about the desired outcome.
It is too late for such questions now.
And you don't want to let the team down.
Remember that boy on the ground?
So, Quick!
Push the button!
Against the rules?
No.
We have a special rule.
Besides, They broke the rules first.
And They broke them much harder.

So, push it!
Push it!
Push it!
Push it!
There.
Time for supper.

your poet addresses the shade of john dillinger
(or, the myth of john dillinger's dick)

Those chubby, breastfed cheeks belie
the drill bits hanging from your soulless eyes.
And every child learns the myth of your penis
swimming like some dead frog in formaldehyde.
Is it true that my grandfather's dust bowl sweat
was taxed to preserve that lawless pickle?
Are schoolboys gawking at your legendary tool
at the very moment I'm making this poem,
in some velvet-roped Smithsonian hall?

Well, John, it was money well spent. Though,
I have no illusions about you being at the bottom;
an ignorant, murdering rube - sweet cheeks notwithstanding.
But there are wars and rumors of wars now, John, and
we've run out of dusty back roads down which
a human being might make a break for it.
The progeny of your desperate dick have tattooed
the palm prints of dead children on their backs
and carry the hungry teeth of disease within them.
We have become a nation of the fattened famished,
led to our slaughter by obese ballerina toddlers.
The wind of our bleating voices is lifting the sea now
and a killing God is rising like a fist of smoke above the city,
but I just keep thinking:
if we can reach down into the darkness, John,
and if we can still find your outlaw member swimming like some
freak fish glowing in the depths of our numbness,
maybe there's a chance, John - just a chance, that
we might carve ourselves a shoe-polished wooden gun
and break the fuck out of this crummy joint.

my body is a vacant building

Somewhere in the bone city
my body is a vacant building
scheduled for demolition.
My soul is a committee
of escaped mental patients
whose paperwork has been lost.

No one is looking for them.

Officially they do not exist.

They wolf meals of shoplifted bread,
squatting in my cold empty rooms.

During the long bone blizzard of their madness
they have learned something about loneliness,
and so my emptiness would be offered up
for any traveler to bed down within my walls
and decorate my halls
with lucid vagrant profanity:
cocks and cunts and tits and balls.

Not the saccharine phrases
hanging like your mother's paps,
by magnets from the refrigerator.
Those are the true curses, friend,
and I would ask that you leave them at the door
for starving feral cats to eat.

Bring only your wounded words inside me.

The words that you would hurl like bricks through placid windows
exploding the rodent stares of human moles like glass.
The words you spit in wet gasps upon your lover's shoulder.
The words you'd say now if you had to do it over.

And the words you never said because
their freight of truth would have wrecked the world.

Bring these inside my condemned, five-story husk
and spray them in snarling black swathes
like bruises in my empty rooms.
And do not mind the mental patients
in their stained hospital gowns
wandering the halls like ghosts.

I will count it as a kindness
if you find refuge here.
If the curses and the names
and the frozen black shouts of loneliness
testify in their stillness.

Until the day when a fat crane operator
with locally famous B.O.
spits cigar fragments onto the floor of his beat-up rig,
and plays his black-knobbed levers like a virtuoso;
sending a steel ball crashing
through my rotting walls

and mental patients

spray out

like bowling pins.

lines addressed to the stoics

"We hold ... that sages are happy just because they are virtuous, and can be happy even on the rack."
- Lawrence C. Becker, A New Stoicism

You can be happy on the rack, the stoics used to say.
But what if the asteroid belt consists of millions of slapped heads
tumbling in the perfect vacuum of dead love?
What if you can't be happy *off* the rack? Huh?
Cat got yer tongue, mister dead stoic dude?
Here, don't rend yer toga! I ain't bein' rude.

Look, I know you were just all bummed out
about the Roman empire winding down,
but I'm kinda glad it did, truth to tell.

I think I'd suck donkey dick as a gladiator.

But I just keep thinking about those heads,
each one a stoic sage, hurtling through space,
Set into motion by a small, pissed-off hand.

fragments from the dead elvis mythos

I

Last night while getting my back shaved
by a vintage Raquel Welch replica robot,
I had a very nice talk with dead Elvis.
He drilled through a thousand feet
of congealed boredom just to see me.
Death has decisively solved his weight problem
and though he walks through a daily blizzard
of very hot dead women's panties,
he's still so not over Mama Cass, it's just sad.
He's been sleeping on Tiny Tim's couch
in a suite at the heartbreak hotel.
He's become the Ed McMahon of dead Johnny,
and he stole Sammy Davis' glass eye.
He keeps it in his mouth and pops it out
at unexpected times to look at you.
He's getting up the courage to swallow it,
Shit it out and stick it back in Sammy's head
who hopefully then will explain to him what it saw.

II

Elvis loved the feeling of the casino
at 4:00 am in the morning;
the blue-hair ladies' grim mouths
like shaved poodle sphincters
gripping weary cigarettes
a-dangle like post-coital dicks
as he ventured from his suite
disguised in one of Cass's wigs
on an impromptu quest
for the ham sandwich of her dreams.

III

Behind the mildewed shower curtain
where the drunken doctor removes
stubborn leeches the size of garden slugs
from the pulsating brain of fat, dead Elvis
like a machine gun loaded with promises.

IV

I think things started going to shit when Elvis died.
(I remember not giving a fuck so clearly that day).
Or it might have been the day that Mama Cass
choked to death on that goddamn ham sandwich.
If they'd shacked up, maybe things'd be better:
they'd have fallen into a kind of deep fried love
and Elvis could have given Cass the Heimlich,
and Cass could have kept Elvis off of the pills,
and they'd have fucked (there's a visual!),
and had a big fat baby who would now rule the earth,
and we'd all be walking 'round in blue suede shoes...
or not.

lines at midnight to the NSA

Dear NSA thank you for watching over us.

Dear NSA I would support letting you out of those computers to walk around sometimes.

Dear NSA eat shit- just kidding don't send out a drone.

Dear NSA thanks for listening, I'm kinda lonely right now.

Dear NSA if America were a person, you would be the brain but what would be the heart?

Dear NSA as the brain you should know this.

Dear NSA that's some mighty big data you have there.

Dear NSA you know our every thought... just like Jesus.

Dear NSA please explain us to ourselves, maybe in a groovy pop song.

Dear NSA my thoughts are like playful dolphins trapped in green jello sometimes.

Dear NSA have you ever kissed a girl?

Dear NSA don't worry so much buddy.

Dear NSA wizzle-walla-bing-bang-zip-dang-do.

Dear NSA we probably mainly bore the crap out of you, sorry.

Dear NSA what does our confusion taste like?

Dear NSA is your deepest fear the end of war?

Dear NSA I'm going to sleep now, but you probably knew that.

lines to a legal entity
(Thanks to Bill)

It doesn't matter what you think I said,
or if I come to zero in your sight.
My words might put a landmine in your head.

I've been shouting till my face is red,
trying to exhume a bone of light.
But it never mattered what I said.

I know you think I'm less alive than dead.
The way you chew my soul out isn't right.
I want to stick a landmine in your head.

And you might think its praise you hear instead,
twisting necks there on your pinstripe height,
pulling legs off every word I said.

It will sear your brain like molten lead
and lie there silent, waiting, silver-bright,
this landmine that I'm putting in your head.

And you will touch it sometime in your bed.
Your shrieks will clog the gutters of the night.
You never listened to a word I said,
and now you've got this landmine in your head.

thoughts in a coffee shop in sedona, arizona

A tungsten bird calls the first light of morning.
A mechanical dog lifts its glass-eyed head.
The shrink-wrapped man puts away the night.
The electric woman rises up in her bed.

Now our insectile voices emerge
like iron shavings falling from our mouths,
into the hungry gaping steel beaks
of predator drones thinking about sex.

Do not tell me that you are different,
that your heart is not another contrivance
that love leaves no stains on your driveway
that this God of yours doesn't need a ring job.

It was all set in motion like some boney clock.
On the day that soldiers rode up on bronze camels
with the words of the God-king from the city below
contained in scratches on a plate of baked mud

The plains were littered with the stone genitals we made,
we knew that the dark magic was already old.
We should have stayed in our huts of diesel mammoth hide
and enacted once more the coupling of beasts.

lines on occupy salt lake city
(a belated eulogy)

Hey poets, let's come clean:
we don't give a flying fuck about the truth.
We are not unbiased journalists of the soul,
let's admit.

But now, a word from our sponsor, VAGINAS!

(actually the correct plural should be
vaginae, but vaginas is accepted and
sounds less pedantic)

Remember when a giant one opened up in a park in
downtown Salt Lake City? And a drunk homeless
man tried to fuck it and fell in? But the
vagina turned out to be a wormhole
to an alternate world ruled by telepathic dogs
who considered it a civic duty to castrate
their human pets. So the guy got de-balled
which freaked him out at first but afterward
he was kinda glad, as though a deep madness
had been lifted, and was also glad
that his dog owner kept him fed and groomed
and even gave him a toy, remember that?

Neither do I but it's a better story than the truth.

The truth sucked at being a story.

Vaginas played only a supporting role,
although I'm sure they stole a scene or two.

No telepathic dogs, no reversal of pet roles.

Just some people hoping this might be it.

Just a man nodding off hopeful
for the first time in a long, long time,
and then not waking up.

And the people driving by,
shaking their heads,
they were right of course.

The truth is, nothing's going to change.

Until one day, it does.

hart and me among the fishes

When I learned that the atmosphere was called a fluid
I promptly soiled myself with a babe's hedonic smile.
Now I know why I am sitting next to a monkfish!
I turn to him with protruding, bloodshot eyes.
"We are creatures of the fucking deep!" I shout.
The monkfish merely gapes incomprehension.

Well, that's fine for you, Mr. Mouth-With-a-Tail!
I'll go looking for my old drinking buddy, Hart Crane.
It is mathematically certain that he swims among us.
He is now a balloonfish made of syringe needles.
I will find him swimming the streets behind sailors.

Oh teacher of my youth, companion of my loneliness!
I never really got half of your shit, but I loved to read it anyway-
Creamy verbal froth over a bottomless ocean of lust.
I always wondered what poems you would have written
If The Bridge could have carried freight of *your* truth;
If this land had been free enough to let you speak it.

But no.

You understood that this America of which you sang
would just as soon gut you like the fish you became.

You'll be glad to know that things have changed a bit,
though it didn't come of shouting modernist stanzas.
But that sea of oblivion in which you sought final refuge
has come to engulf us all, my dead carp friend.
We've become submerged in a rising sea of futility,
Glimpsing each other's scaled silver shimmer
through the translucent, green murk of it,
Enmeshed in tentacular streams of data.

We can see the edge of the world from here, old friend.
The point beyond which all is irreversibly fucked,
and we just float here staring at it
with our blank fish eyes,
our sucker-mouths working in a spastic rhythm.
We've all opted for the same out as you did,
and maybe, in a way, for the very same reason;
but unlike yours - and the revolution -
Our suicide will definitely be televised.

an unrare bird

Flail.

Flailing.

Flailer.

One who flails.

The principle visible symptom of the disease was frequent, involuntary flailing.

Rather than leave conspicuous space on either side of him, the caterer's staff were instructed to place name cards for imaginary people next to him and to pretend that they were no-shows, in order to create ample room for his unpredictable fits of flailing.

That night he began flailing in his sleep. When he awoke he found himself staring at his own face in the bathroom mirror, his arms flapping spastically as though he was a large, crazy bird.

"I am a crazy bird," he told himself. "A rather large, featherless, flightless, flailing, crazy bird."

Valiantly making the best of things, he glared at himself with merciless, predatory bird eyes; the fierce eyes of a hawk.

His head moved suddenly, as though sensing distant prey.

Flailing, flailing, flailing...

sixes

Instead of working I am writing you this poem.
Is that a tattoo that I see upon your tit?
These men in masks are here to fumigate my home
with cubic meters of a very poison gas.
The concept you are reaching for is corporate shit,
although a corporation doesn't have an ass.

You shouldn't read this poem until the fumes abate.
Killing vermin isn't all that great a job,
But even so, you shouldn't come an hour late
to rid the rooms inside this poem of bugs and rats
and leave the door ajar with moisture on the knob.
To get a better gig you'll have to hide the tatts.

The skeletons of rats are systems made of bone.
The bodies of the bugs are very dry and light.
The rat bones hate you now and won't leave you alone.
The bugs are bombed-out Humvees from a tiny war
Tattoo your tit with shit and guzzle gas all night.
You've been sold out, it doesn't matter anymore.

If fear were poison gas we'd all be very dead.
Your skeleton would snap closed like a steel trap.
This poem is snapping closed so get this through your head:
It's sixes what you ink into your poor white chest.
The bone committee will not listen to your rap;
You're going to fall in line and scuffle with the rest.

You did what was required, you snapped right into place.
You wore your mask and sprayed the gas where you were told.
You lost your heart, you lost your mind, you lost the race,
and thanks a heap but now it's sixes what you do.
It's been a sixes game since you were none year old.
I wouldn't put you in a poem that isn't true.

We trained you up a little for our constant war.
There were sixes on the beast you went to kill.
But now you're back and we can't use you anymore.
So go ahead and schlepp some drinks for us instead,
and write it in your flesh if you can find the will:
It's sixes if you live. Sixes if you're dead.

the little-known but true inventor of strawberry soda
(a street-corner rant)

Attend me now oh long dead father with the brown hard-angled
    pants.
Unsung concocter of the fizzy lifeblood of a psychopathic nation.
Discrete but ardent coveter of smooth-groined third grade teachers
    with wire hair.
Pipe-smoking cold war lab tech deep in the paranoid guts of corpo-
    rate America,
how could one not envy the resoluteness of thy pale and deeply cleft
    chin
as you plied your dark trade in the basement of our publicly traded
    whore mother
whose CEO was a cum-stained cardboard Jesus with moving robot
    eyes
and from whose sanctified odorless corporate cunt issued all later
    corporations?

Of course you were working late, oh standardly groomed one.
While at home your faithful love-match wrapped your supper up in
    foil
no microwaves yet in this decade of genius,
when fag mathematicians deep-throated early computers
and donated their vacuum tube balls to the state,
and Ginsberg put his queer shoulder to the wheel,
and I was fucking born if you'd like to know.

I sing you standing in your immaculate lab coat
your head inclined slightly as you peer into the beaker.
Oh clean-shaven father it was then that you decanted
the beautiful red Jesus-jizz into a test tube,
and then you smoked 'em cause you had 'em to give it time to cool.
And then you took a taste of it and knew that it would rule!
Pure conjugal bliss in a chemical equation!
True dick-hardening crazy love in substance form!
Simple and deadly and effective like insecticide

except the insect here is your fucking frown.
The insect is your lack of hard-on.
The insect is your bad attitude.
The insect is your problem with authority.

And let us not forget the importance of fizz!

For this was not the ass-gas of single-celled animals
drowning in a rising sea of their own piss, no,
this CO_2 came from clean chemical reactions in huge buildings
proceeding 24/7 with workers arriving at midnight with sagging faces,
in the vast asphalt fields walking reflected in oil stains
by the bruise-colored light of a moon through dark clouds
and the precious gas they made was stored in steel bottles
And forklifted onto truck after truck
which then flowed out into the nation by night
like blood flowing into the wrinkles on a face.
Bottles clinking together in the jostling of the freeway
through Oklahoma, Texas, Colorado, Ohio,
every corner of a nation thirsty for red sweet bubbling delusion.
Lest it wake up in the grey light of a concrete block motel room
and see its reflection in the mirror,
and walk out to pawn its watch for the price of a drink.
Thank you oh slim-waisted dickless plastic dad for giving us
the blood of another self to keep us from ourselves.

Oh there had been strawberry soda before of course
perpetrated by jerks in the opiated hinterland
with gritted teeth and serial-killer dead eyes.
In roadside stands where the girl from the next town allowed
the pale hams of her thighs to emerge from her cotton dress
glistening with 100 proof sweat.

Oh we see shadows going back in time, oh yes
inklings of the sugared bubbling milk from the cast iron tits of histo-
    ry,
at every turn a new puddle of blood begins to fizz on second glance

drawings on the walls of lost buried caves.
Everywhere hands dipped in red and pressed out
as if to stop the advance of reality with sticky sweet strawberry palms.

That the stuff was first squirted from the hermaphroditic paps
of your spastic psycho God is easily said of course
but wrong wrong wrong.
Oh yes, God piled up the mud on the bank of the blood-red river
mumbling to himself like a lunatic
crazy from loneliness.
He blew his carrion-reeking breath into the mud and made a man
but then he stood the fuck back and let *us* make the world
and the bombs and the madness and the piles of stinking corpses
and the essence of this berry too,
as proven by the glistening glass tube in your hand.

Oh my people, my people!
When did we forsake the vision of gentle red bubbling sweetness that
        was ours
exploding like a nuclear wet dream in our dazzling white fruit-of-the-
        looms?
Was it the threat of annihilation that so focused our minds?
that released the carbonated menses of our colossal whore society?

None of the rumors were true of course.
None of the foul lies.

It was not the diluted blood of lynched niggers infused with CO_2,
this was not the strange fruit Billy Holiday sang about.
It was not the carbonated discharge of Texas high school cheerleaders
collected by the IRS as a federal tax on righteousness.
It was not the squeezings of the severed testicles of southern convicts
offering up their balls in lieu of hard chain gang labor.
Nor was the true purpose of our numerous wars
to provide the red juice for this our holy beverage.
It was not the fizzified blood of a million murdered children.

No, my people listen not to the puny limp-dicked detractors
devouring the multifaceted pewter pig of conspiracy.
Our neck-tied father's gift to us was none of those things, oh no.
It was the high-grade distillate of an advanced God-eating paranoid
    culture in full flower
hiding in its bedroom waiting to be spanked,
jerking off to the bra section of a Sunday paper insert.
Why oh people would you reject this?
Why would you look under Barbie's skirt?
Why would you look down the barrel of a loaded history?

Oh give me the top-shelf stuff my father
in the dusty bottles saved from the beginning.
Tell me once more of this heaven
where God lies down like a great bitch with infinite dugs
from which the millions of the righteous hang for all eternity
sucking the delicious red bubbling milk from her scab-nippled glands.

Be with me father as I sit across from the beautiful woman
and take her small hand in mine on a milk-white tablecloth.
Guide my curling tongue oh wise one, as it invades the gill-like
    fringes
at the tentative welcoming frontier of the red sweetness I require.
Oh walk thou with me now oh father; as I make my pilgrimage
across the piss-stained concrete overpass into the dying city;
as I hose the shit and the blood and the anguish
from the floor and the walls of the graffiti-covered blind alley
and on the milk run greyhound at 1:00 AM;
when the lady from Hoboken begins to snore
and the sad junky chick finally nods off as the awol marine
slips his fingers down the top of her jeans;
and the headlights of a passing truck
turn the driver's shaved head into an asteroid
deep, deep in outer space.

too many daves

It was Dave's misfortune to have come down with the same disease as everyone else.

Then he died.

When he came to his senses he wasn't experiencing any extreme pain.

He assumed he was in heaven.

He was wrong.

He was in the disputed territory between heaven and hell, called 'Helen'.

In addition to being disputed territory, Helen was a middle-aged alcoholic woman who lived in Clearfield, Utah.

Dave's afterlife would consist of being married to Helen.

One night, as Dave and Helen drank beer from cans and ate frozen pot pies on TV trays while gazing spellbound at a television program about people like themselves being arrested, it suddenly occurred to Helen that there were far too many daves in her world.

Far, far too many.

"Of course you wouldn't know this," Helen told Dave, "but I am named after a tragic figure, celebrated in song and story, on behalf of whose face a thousand ships were launched. And you are just a.... dave."

"Well, Dav-ID, if you want to get technical about it," said Dave, "of biblical fame, of course. Plucker of lutes, composer of psalms, slayer of Goliaths, bedder of Bathsheba. Are you going to finish that pie?"

"Nonsense. You are only a dave, Dave. My father was a dave, and my oldest brother. My first husband. I recall lying on my back, pinching out dave after dave. And now you. Something has gone wrong. I am under a curse of daves."

"Well, imagine my disappointment when, after dying of an entirely typical disease, I find myself consigned to you."

"You speak gibberish, Dave. And you may not have the remainder of this pie. I would rather throw it out."

"Furthermore, as a little reflection would reveal to you," continued Dave with spinning, pinwheel eyes as he took out his average-sized penis, "with my typical disease and banal death and forgettable name I must now commit the utterly predictable act."

"Murder?"

"Yes. More specifically, murder combined with sex. I will fuck you to death."

"And that is to be your weapon?"

"Correct. Well – this and, if need be, that lamp over there."

"Too many daves."

"You've come to your last dave, Helen."

"Thank you, Dave."

"My pleasure entirely, Helen."

"But Dave?"

"Yes, Helen?"

"Oh, nothing, Just...dave.

dave.   122

dave dave

davedavedavedaaaaaaaaaaaaaaaaaaaaaaaaaaaaaaaaaa

vid."

About the Author

Kurt Rasmussen is currently at large somewhere near Ogden, Utah, where he continues to elude capture through various acts of subterfuge. He makes frequent forays into the city. If sighted, do not attempt to engage him. Contact the proper authorities.